Off the Grid

Off the Grid

Lesley Choyce

orca soundings

ORCA BOOK PUBLISHERS

Library and Archives Canada Cataloguing in Publication

Choyce, Lesley, 1951–, author
Off the grid / Lesley Choyce.
(Orca soundings)

Issued in print and electronic formats.
ISBN 978-1-4598-0926-0 (pbk.).—ISBN 978-1-4598-0928-4 (pdf).—
ISBN 978-1-4598-0929-1 (epub)

I. Title. II. Series: Orca soundings
PS8555.H668O34 2015   jc813'.54   c2014-906677-5
c2014-906678-3

First published in the United States, 2015
Library of Congress Control Number: 2014952062

Summary: Homeschooled and naïve, Cody must attempt to fit in and
stand up for what he believes when he moves to the city.

*Orca Book Publishers is dedicated to preserving the environment and has
printed this book on Forest Stewardship Council® certified paper.*

Orca Book Publishers gratefully acknowledges the support for its publishing
programs provided by the following agencies: the Government of Canada through
the Canada Book Fund and the Canada Council for the Arts,
and the Province of British Columbia through the BC Arts Council
and the Book Publishing Tax Credit.

Cover image by Getty Images

ORCA BOOK PUBLISHERS
PO Box 5626, Stn. B
Victoria, BC Canada
V8R 6S4

ORCA BOOK PUBLISHERS
PO Box 468
Custer, WA USA
98240-0468

www.orcabook.com
Printed and bound in Canada.

18 17 16 15 • 4 3 2 1

For my brother, Gordon Choyce

Chapter One

It all happened so quickly. When my dad got sick, we had to move to the city so he could get treatment in the hospital. None of us had seen this coming. Especially me.

So I traded the wilderness for the city. My home for some crappy apartment. My life alone in the woods with my family for this insanity of city life and going to a big high school. Nothing could have prepared me for it. Nothing. It was like a bad dream. But it wasn't a dream. It was real. Too real.

On my first day at Citadel High, I felt like I was on another planet. I was a freak, a sixteen-year-old freak who had grown up in the woods. *Off the grid*, as my father liked to say. The clothes I wore were secondhand, given to me by the Cancer Society, which was taking care of us. My regular clothes would have made me stand out even more than I already did. I hated what I had to wear. My mom said I didn't have a choice. I had to go to school. My dad wasn't well enough to continue with my homeschooling, and my mom said she was too upset to help me with my schoolwork.

So I arrived at school on my own, first thing in the morning on our third day in town. The hallways were filled with kids shouting and bumping into each other. They all looked at me and they could tell I was lost and hopeless in this zoo. I'd been lost before in the forest, but it was never like this. I could always find my way home. The wind, the sun, even the birds could guide me. But here I had no guides. This was *lost* lost.

And I hated to admit it, but I was scared.

I didn't even know where I was supposed to go or what I was supposed to do. I was about to bail on the whole crappy thing when someone walked up to me. A big guy, maybe a head taller than me and thick around the neck. He stood in front of me and just looked at me, a smirk on his face. "Holy Christ," he said, staring at me. "Where did you come from?" He sniffed the air. "When was the last time you had a bath?"

Some other students were watching. They began to laugh. I wanted to run. I just didn't know where to run to.

Then this girl who had pink hair and a piece of metal stuck across her nose walked up and jabbed an elbow in the gut of the tough guy in front of me. "Leave him alone, Austin," she said. "I know you can't help being a jerk, but lighten up."

I couldn't help but notice she had some words painted on the back of her neck: *Wild at Heart*. I think maybe she scared me more than big Austin, but at least she was trying to help.

Austin snorted once, just like a bear I had met in the woods one summer. Then shot me a look that said this wasn't over. But he left.

The girl looked at me. "You must be autistic or something,"

"What?" I asked.

"Oh, so you *do* speak English. Got a name?"

"Cody," I said. "Cody Graham."

Kids were still looking at me, at us.

She didn't seem to care, but I felt like I had bugs crawling on me.

"I gotta get to class. Where do you need to be?"

"I don't know. I've never been here before."

"I'll take you to the office."

"Thanks."

In the office, I saw a kid with a nosebleed and a girl who was crying. She kept repeating, "But I lost my iPhone," over and over.

There was this loud noise and I jumped. The girl shook her head. "It's just the bell, Moonboy. I gotta go. See that guy in there?" She pointed to a small inner office. "That's Mr. Costanzo, one of the vice-principals. Talk to him. He'll know what to do." She squeezed my arm and then left.

5

I stood in the doorway to his office. Mr. Costanzo was sitting at a desk, staring at a pile of papers. He finally looked up. "What?" he asked.

"I don't know. That girl said I should talk to you."

"So talk. Who are you? I don't recognize you."

"Cody Graham," I said. "I was told I had to come here. To go to school."

Then something seemed to click. He smiled. "Oh, right. The kid from the woods."

"Yeah," I said. "The kid from the woods."

"Welcome to Citadel High. I looked at the record of work you've been doing on your own. Very impressive. I'll set you up with a schedule and get you into some classes. What do you think of the school so far?"

I just shrugged and tried not to scream.

Chapter Two

Mr. Costanzo rattled off a lot of stuff that I didn't really follow. Then he led me down the empty hallways. We ended up in a room where about thirty kids were sitting at desks in rows. He introduced me to a teacher and left. The teacher told me to take a seat, and the kids all watched as I looked around. I took a seat in the back but had no idea what I was supposed to do or how I was supposed to act.

Austin, the big guy from before, was in this class. He turned around in his seat and gave me a dirty look. The teacher, a tall man with glasses, began speaking and writing words on the board. I didn't know what I was supposed to do, so I just sat there and looked out the window at a maple tree. There was a squirrel in that tree, and the squirrel kept me sane.

And then the bell rang again. Everyone closed their books, packed up and left. I was still sitting there looking at the squirrel when the teacher said, "Didn't you hear the bell? You can leave."

I had no idea where I was supposed to go next. I left and went outside and sat under that tree, wondering what the hell I had been thrown into.

A while later, the bell sounded again and kids started walking out of the school. I saw the girl from the morning coming down the steps. She saw me and waved. I waved back, and she walked over and sat down.

"Cutting classes already, Moonboy? Not good."

"I guess not," I said. I shrugged. "I'm not sure what I am supposed to be doing. She laughed and tapped me on the knee. "No one does. We all just play games. So forget about trying to do what anyone expects. Be yourself. It's Cody, right?"

"Yeah."

"Cody, I'm Alexis, but you can call me Lex."

I nodded. "You can tell I look lost, right? I've just never been any place like this before."

"You mean you've never gone to school?"

"No. I was homeschooled."

"Where are you from?"

"A long way from here."

"I mean, what town?"

"Not a town. Just a place."

"The place must have a name."

"We just called it home."

"That's original." I thought she was going to get up and walk away, but instead she leaned closer. "Okay, now you've got me curious. Tell me what it's like, wherever home is."

I took a deep breath. I had promised myself not to reveal too much about my past life to anyone, but I was so freaked out by this whole new school thing that I felt I needed to explain it to someone. So I told her. "Okay. Up until recently, I lived with my mom and dad a hundred miles east of here. We lived in the woods about twenty miles from the closest road. My parents cleared the land and built the house there about four years before I was born."

"You're kidding, right?"

I shook my head. "My parents were very idealistic. They wanted to live *off the grid*, as they called it."

"No friends even?"

"Just my parents. And they were very cool. They taught me. We had books. I never went to school, but my dad made me work every day on schoolwork."

"But no friends to hang out with, no girlfriend?"

I probably blushed. "Just us."

"If I'd had to have no contact with anyone but my parents, I would have killed myself long ago."

"It wasn't like that. We had a good life. We had a wind generator and solar panels. So we could listen to music, and we had light. Woodstove for heating and cooking. My dad said that if everyone lived like we lived, it would solve most of the problems of the world. We weren't hurting anyone or anything, and he taught me that was important. We saw other people when we came to town for supplies once a month. We visited some of my mom's family a few times. It wasn't complete isolation."

"What did you do for food?"

"We had a garden. We grew our own food. And we hunted."

Something changed in the way she looked at me. "Wait a minute. Did you say you hunted?"

"Yeah. We had a bow and arrows and a couple of rifles. I learned to shoot a gun when I was about twelve."

She seemed angry. "You mean you killed animals yourself."

I nodded. "I only killed a creature that we would use for food—spruce grouse, rabbits, deer, mostly. I got to be really good at it. And my dad taught me the proper way to gut and skin the carcass and preserve the meat."

Alexis stood up. Her attitude toward me had suddenly changed. "You killed and ate rabbits and deer?" She was almost shouting. I didn't know what to say.

She shook her head, turned and walked off. I was stunned. Other kids were looking at me and laughing.

I wanted to run, but I saw that guy, Mr. Costanzo, heading my way, walking really fast. He must have been watching from inside the school. He came right up to me. He must have seen the confusion on my face, because he said in a friendly voice, "Don't worry. You're not the first person to feel the wrath of Alexis."

"Can I go home now?" I asked. I didn't really mean *home*, just the crappy apartment where my mom and I were staying while my dad was in the hospital.

"I really think you should finish the day. Look, I know you missed some classes, so I found a student with the same schedule as you. He said you could shadow him for the rest of the day."

I didn't know what else to do. So I said okay.

Chapter Three

Mr. Costanzo led me to the library and introduced me to a black kid sitting at a table and reading a magazine. "Cody, this is DeMarco."

DeMarco smiled and held out his hand. I shook it. Mr. Costanzo said, "I'll let you two get to know each other. I've got work to do," and then he left.

DeMarco looked me up and down and shook his head. "I don't mean to be rude, but you gotta get some new threads."

"Threads?"

"Clothes. Look, I know Mr. C. says you've been living in the woods and all, but if you don't want to look like 1962, you better get with the program."

Just then something on the table buzzed, and DeMarco looked at it. It was a mobile phone. There were words on a tiny screen. DeMarco nodded and started tapping it with his fingers. I was amazed how kids seemed to spend so much time on their phones. I had never had one.

DeMarco read the look on my face. He smiled again. "Tell me you've never seen someone texting before."

I shrugged.

"Never had a cell phone?"

"I never had a reason to use a phone."

That made DeMarco laugh. But it wasn't a nasty laugh. He gave me a gentle slap on the shoulder. "Well, this is going to be interesting. Welcome to the twenty-first century, cowboy. I'm just gonna have to bring you up to speed. Time to get your white ass to your next class, Code."

I decided to keep my mouth shut for the rest of the day, fearing I'd say something wrong, like I'd done with Alexis. The plan worked well enough until the final bell rang.

"End of the day, Code," DeMarco announced. "Let freedom ring."

But as we were walking out the school door, we passed Alexis, with a couple of other girls. Alexis gave me a look like I was something on the sole of her shoe and pushed past us.

DeMarco had no idea what was going on. "Just keep walking, bro."

We walked in silence for a couple of blocks before he asked, "What was that all about? How'd you make girl enemies on your first day of school?"

I tried to explain as best I could. DeMarco's eyes went wide. "So let me get this straight. You meet a nice girl like Alexis and try to impress her by telling her you're good at shooting bunny rabbits and stripping the skin off a deer?"

DeMarco registered that look in my eyes. I guess it had been my trademark look all day—dazed and confused and not having a clue. "Codeman," he said. "We've got some serious work to do. Serious work."

But DeMarco had a part-time job at a coffee shop that he had to get to. He said goodbye and left me on my own to walk down a city street full of busy people, all walking and talking on their little phones or tapping away on them like it was the most important thing in the world.

I almost got hit by a couple of cars while crossing the street, and a few people yelled at me. I longed for the quiet and solitude of the forest. I just wanted to sit by the little brook and listen to it. I suddenly realized, too, just how hungry and thirsty I was.

I saw a fountain in front of a big building, with a pool of water around it. I leaned over the concrete edge and drank deeply from the pool. It tasted different from the well water at home and the stream I sometimes drank from when I was in the forest. But it helped.

Once again I noticed people looking at me in an odd way. What was I doing wrong? The more I looked at their faces, the more I realized they thought I was crazy or had something wrong with me. One young man with long hair walked by and nudged me and said, "Easy on it, my friend. I think you're takin' the wrong drugs." But I had no idea what he meant.

In spite of all that, I took another drink from the pool. When I looked up and around, I realized I had no idea which way to go to get back to the apartment. I was totally lost in a city I didn't understand. And I wanted to cry.

Chapter Four

My mother has always said that crying doesn't help, but it also doesn't hurt. And I had cried plenty of times in my life, sometimes in pain, sometimes out of loneliness. But I wouldn't cry now. It was clear I was in a world I knew nothing about. A world where people walked around like zombies staring at their phones and where you were not supposed to drink water in public. I didn't know how to get back to the apartment. And there was no way I would walk back to the school.

I sat on the edge of the pool, remembering what my father had said about getting lost in the woods. *When you get lost, stay lost for the time being. Stay put. Don't just wander. It will make things worse. Sit down and think. Come up with a plan.*

I had my head down, staring at the concrete. And then this old guy sat down beside me. He had a smell about him. Nothing I was familiar with. Not body odor, but something else. Something strong.

"Looks like you need some kind of help," he said.

I nodded and looked at him. He was maybe sixty, unshaven, and in old clothes like my dad would wear chopping wood. He had a bottle in a brown paper bag, and he held it out. "Want some?"

I didn't know what it was, but I accepted the bottle and took a sip. The liquid burned like hell, and I spit it out.

The guy looked offended. "Shouldn't waste good sauce," he said, putting a cap on the bottle and shoving it into his pocket. I was coughing and trying to get my breath. "Just trying to ease the pain, kiddo."

I took a gulp of air. "I'm lost," I said. "Think you can help me find my way home?"

"Sure," he said. "I know all about lost. Been that way most of my life. I'd go home too if I knew where home was, but I don't. But I bet I can get you where you need to go. Where you from anyway?"

So I gave him the short version of my tale. Wide-eyed, he pulled out the bottle and took a deep gulp, but he didn't offer it to me this time.

"I'm Ernest, by the way. Ernest by name but not by nature." He laughed at his little joke. "I'm not exactly your guardian angel, buddy. But let's figure this out. You say your father's in the hospital, and they put you and your mom up somewhere."

"Yeah, a tall building."

"Lots of them around. But let's head toward the hospital and see if you recognize anything."

So we started walking. He had a bit of a limp, so we went slow. And he was right. About twenty minutes later we were circling the streets around Regional General Hospital when I recognized an old, dirty brick building. "That's it," I said. "You want to come in and meet my mom?"

He smiled and shook his head. "No. I got places to go, people to meet. I'm just happy you found your way home."

"Thanks."

"No problem." He turned and I watched as he hobbled off.

My mom was happy to see me. She could read me like a book. "Rough day?"

"Yeah. Rough day."

She gave me a sad look. "Maybe we made a mistake raising you like we did."

"I love everything about the way I grew up," I said. "I want to go back."

"We never expected this would happen to your father. We have to stay here for now. He'll get better, and then we'll go home."

But I had this gut feeling that even if we could go back home, something had changed, and it could never quite be the same. I told my mom about school, about the fountain and about Ernest.

"Let's go visit your father," she said.

We walked the couple of blocks to the hospital and went inside. My mom took me to the cancer ward, and we walked into a room with several beds. Behind some curtains, my dad was sitting up in bed. He had tubes going into his arms, and he looked pale and weak.

"How was the first day at school?"

"Not so bad," I lied.

"It'll get better," he said. My mom was fidgeting, adjusting the bedcovers and then running her fingers through his hair. "Hey. School, city, forest, whatever. It's all about your inner resources."

I'd heard a million of these little speeches before, had grown tired of them but had them memorized. And right now I didn't mind. It was good to hear him say stuff like that. "I know, Dad."

"Just use your instincts and your survival skills."

"There were no wolves or bears at school, Dad."

He smiled. "Sure there were. You saw them. Just keep your distance and stay downwind of them." He coughed and closed his eyes for a second. I could see he was in some kind of pain.

"We'll all get through this," he said to me. "And then we can go home. We gotta get some firewood cut and split before winter."

My mom leaned over him and gave him a hug. I did the same. Then we sat for a while in silence, listening to the other sounds in the hospital.

Chapter Five

My mom said I had no choice. I had to go back to school. So I went.

DeMarco was waiting for me outside the school. "Good to see you, Code. The look's improving. Not much, but it shows some hope."

I was wearing my father's old hooded sweatshirt, the one he used to wear when he worked in the garden on cold days. I had seen other kids at school wearing something like it.

"Ready for day number two?"

"Not really."

"Listen. Just try your best to stay under the radar. Don't draw attention to yourself."

"Easier said than done."

"Listen. I know the ropes."

"You mean because you're black?"

"Yeah, but I'm also gay."

I must have looked puzzled.

"I like other guys."

I shrugged. I understood what he was saying. It was just that he was the first gay person I had ever met, and I was trying to sort things out and make sense of the new information. I figured my best bet was to not overreact to anything that surprised me. But I guess I looked a little stunned.

"I'm assuming you're not of the same persuasion?"

I shook my head.

"Being black and being gay does draw attention to me. People want to get on my case. So I have to learn to deflect the bad stuff. I have to make sure it all bounces off me. Now, if you hang out with me, you're gonna get some of the flak yourself. Might be another strike against you."

"I don't understand."

"Well, first you show up here after crawling out from under a rock. Then you piss off some white-girl vegetarian by talking about hunting. Now you hang out with an openly gay guy."

"I still don't get it."

"Well, if you hang out with me, people will start thinking you're gay too. So what we have here is a gay Bambi killer from the sticks."

It took a while for it all to sink in, but when it did, I started to laugh. The laughing felt really good. I guess I was a bit loud, because that got us some eyeball attention. But then DeMarco started to laugh as well.

And I felt that maybe my second day of school wasn't going to be so bad.

I asked DeMarco a few more questions about what he meant by "under the radar," and it began to sink in. "So what you're saying is that I need to be under the radar but not completely off the grid."

He grinned and said, "Now I think you're starting to get the hang of it. Pretty soon we'll be able to shake those pinecones out of your hair and you're gonna fit right in."

With a bit of DeMarco's coaching, I got to all my classes, lay low and made it through the day. After school he had to go to his job, so we parted ways and I promised him I wouldn't drink from any form of public water trough on my way home.

But as I walked off toward the apartment and another visit to the hospital, I heard some people taunting DeMarco. There were three of them—heavyset guys with attitude. I recognized one of them as that creep Austin. DeMarco was trying to get past them, trying to pretend they weren't there, as was his style. They had names for him, names that sounded nasty.

My life in the woods had made me physically strong. You also develop a strange confidence in yourself in tough situations where you need to get physical. Sometimes there's no one around to help you, so you need to be prepared.

Austin and his goons had blocked DeMarco's path as he was walking down the sidewalk. DeMarco was smiling, though, and doing some kind of little dance as he spoke to them, acting like it was all a joke. But then Austin shoved him hard and knocked him down. That's when I decided to get involved. I broke into a run and put two fists in front of me as I smashed into Austin and hammered him until he fell. He hit the ground hard, and I came down on top of him.

I expected Austin's two buddies to come at me so was surprised to find DeMarco grabbing my arms and pulling me up. "No, man. Not like this. Don't be stupid," he said.

Austin's friends hung back, but I could tell they were ready to pounce. "Just a little misunderstanding," DeMarco said to them.

The door of the school opened and a couple of male teachers headed our way.

"C'mon, Cody, let's get out of here." DeMarco tugged at my sleeve.

Austin was on his feet now. He looked at me and then DeMarco. "Faggots!" he shouted, and then he spit on DeMarco.

The teachers were yelling something, but Austin and his two friends were on the run. DeMarco tugged at me again and started running in the opposite direction from the other guys. I ran with him until we were a couple of blocks away, and then we stopped to catch our breath.

"Not the way to play the game, Caveman. Thanks for coming to help, but you fight back against a dog like that and he comes back to bite you another day when you're not looking."

The next day I was summoned into Mr. Costanzo's office. There sat Austin and a cop and a man who introduced himself as Austin's father and pushed a business card into my hand. His old man was a lawyer. You could tell Costanzo didn't like the situation any better than I did. Austin's father did the talking and then turned to the police officer, who seemed as uncomfortable with the whole scene as Costanzo.

The cop said, "Cody, you've been charged with assault. Do you understand what that means?"

I didn't really, but I was thinking of DeMarco, my only friend in this insane place, and I figured if I tried to explain what had happened, he'd get drawn in. "I understand," I said.

The policeman, a kind of no-nonsense guy in his twenties, walked me out to his car and put me in the backseat. Driving me to the police station, he said, "Just doing my job, kid."

I was questioned by a detective in a suit, but I didn't really have anything to say except DeMarco's words: "It was a misunderstanding." In the end, the detective just got frustrated and said, "I'll see if your friend's father is willing to drop the charges. But people will be watching you. You're not off the hook. If this happens again, if there is a pattern here, then we get serious. So keep out of trouble."

The same cop who had brought me in took me home and explained to my mother his version of what had happened. After he left, my mom gave me a hug. Then she looked me in the eye and said, "I'm sorry. We haven't prepared you for any of this. We have to get you back home."

"Don't worry about me," I said. "I can take care of myself. We can't leave until Dad gets better."

But when we visited him at the hospital that night, he was on some kind of medication that made him sleep, and he didn't look like he was on any road to recovery. My mom and I just sat there silently for two hours.

A man in a white coat walked in and introduced himself as Dr. Musgrave. He said that he had taken over my father's case. "I believe we are on the right path here," he said. "It's a pretty serious regimen of medication, but it's necessary. It's going to take some time."

"But he looks worse, not better," my mom said, looking over at the pale face of my father.

"The medication is attacking the cancer cells, but it's also pretty hard on the healthy cells."

Mom looked like she was about to cry.

"How long will he have to stay here?" I asked.

"I can't say," Dr. Musgrave answered. "We have to wait to see if the treatment is working."

"What if it doesn't work?" I asked.

"Then we try something else," he said. It wasn't the answer I was looking for.

Dr. Musgrave got up to go. He looked at me and then at my mother. "I won't lie to you. He may be in for a rough ride.

Lesley Choyce

He's going to need both of you to be strong." And then he left.

I wanted to express the anger and confusion I was feeling, but I didn't have the words to do it. I wanted to find someone or something to blame for making my dad sick and ruining our lives. But I didn't know who or what. So I ended up blaming myself.

Chapter Six

When I left the apartment the next morning, I decided not to go to school. I figured it might be a way to avoid more trouble. Instead, I found my way to the public library and sat down by the water fountain out front. I watched as people hurried by. Everyone seemed so unconnected to the world around them. Some were talking on cell phones, some were texting, and most just seemed in a rush to get somewhere. I didn't see a whole lot of smiles in that crowd. It wasn't my world, and it was a world I really didn't want to be part of.

No one looked at me. I played a game of trying to make eye contact with people, but as soon as they saw me looking at them, they looked away quickly. And then I started thinking about my dad. We were here because of him, because of his cancer. I wasn't sure I trusted Dr. Musgrave or anyone else at the hospital. Maybe we were doing the wrong thing. Maybe we should just get the hell out of here, go back home and let my dad heal there. Up until now, we'd been able to cure or recover from any injury or illness that had come our way. Up until now, we'd been able to handle anything on our own.

That's when I noticed someone lying on his side, asleep on a wooden bench.

I got up and walked over, circled the bench. Yep. It was Ernest. Maybe I should have just let him sleep, but I wasn't sure he was okay. So I touched him on the shoulder, and his body jerked. He sat up and looked around, dazed and uncertain.

"Ernest," I said. "Sorry, man. I was just checking to see if you were okay."

Ernest blinked a few times and then shook his head. He focused on my face and took a breath. "Cody, right?"

"Yeah. You okay?"

Ernest sat up. "I haven't been okay in years. But thanks for asking."

"You slept here last night?"

"I think so."

"Weren't you cold?"

"Of course I was cold." He hawked up some phlegm, leaned over and spit on the ground. "Hey, why aren't you in school?"

So I told him about the trouble I had gotten myself into.

"Yep. Trouble will find you. It always does. Probably nothing you can do about it but be prepared for it."

"You sound like my father," I said and then told him about my visit to my dad and what the doctor had said.

"That's why you have to be strong for your old man. That's why you need to go back to school."

It seemed like an odd sort of thing to say, coming from this guy. But he was probably right.

"So you made an enemy," Ernest continued. "We all do that sometimes. You'll need to be ready to do what needs to be done if your enemy persists."

"I'm just going to try to avoid him."

"Good plan. But have a backup. Now get your ass to school." It was an order, not mere advice.

I smiled. "Okay," I said. He was right. I didn't know where else to go anyway. So I walked to Citadel High and waited for the bell to ring. I checked my schedule and then walked the crowded hallway until I found my English class. DeMarco smiled and waved when I entered the room. "I was worried, Caveman. I thought you'd got lost again in the urban jungle."

I decided not to tell him about the meeting in Costanzo's office or about the police. That was my problem, not his.

When noon rolled around, DeMarco said he had to go home to check on his mom, who wasn't feeling well. So I sat down in the noisy cafeteria, but I didn't have a lunch or any money to buy anything. I watched as kids dumped barely eaten meals into the trash and thought about grabbing something from there. But I knew it would only draw more attention to me. More of the wrong kind of attention.

I saw Alexis walking my way and started to stand. I didn't want any of whatever she'd have to say. But before I could get moving, she sat down across from me. "Sit," she said. "Just sit down, Cody." Her voice was insistent. So I sat down and waited for her to pounce.

"I heard about yesterday," she said. "I heard you got into a fight."

I shrugged and waited for a lecture about nonviolence.

"I heard you stood up for DeMarco."

"Sort of."

"Not too many kids take on Austin or his buddies Jacob and Todd. They're like the local mafia."

"Unfortunately, it got me in trouble with Costanzo and even the police."

"That's not fair," she said.

"Guess it's just the way it is."

She looked at me in a completely different way now. More like the girl who first introduced herself to me. "Cody, I'm sorry about the other day.

"That's okay."

"Can we still be friends?"

"Sure."

The bell was ringing. "See you around," she said. "Just don't tell me any more stories about shooting deer or skinning rabbits."

Chapter Seven

I tried to settle into my classes and make sense of what I was supposed to be learning. My parents had home-schooled me since I was little and had taught me well—writing, history, math, science. Most of it was related to what we needed to know to survive, but my mom had a thing for poetry and novels, so I'd read widely. They had brought a big library of books with them when they moved out to the woods and built our home. Sometimes my dad would pick up new books in town that he'd ordered through the mail.

Most of what I saw in my classrooms didn't make sense. Kids sat at their desks looking bored or sneaking glances at their phones. Teachers lectured about things that didn't seem important—not to me anyway. So I kept to myself and tried to roll with it. Mostly I worried about my father and wondered how we'd ever get back to our old life.

DeMarco walked with me between classes. He seemed to be well liked by many other kids and introduced me to some of them. I never knew what to say. My social skills were a bit lacking. But I found myself looking at girls. I sure liked looking at girls, and I guess it showed. DeMarco noticed. "Yep. Definitely not gay," he said.

And I found myself thinking about Alexis. I was glad she liked me again. Lesson learned. Best not to say too much about the world I had come from. Better to try to fit in. I can do this, I said to myself. But what I really wanted was for my father to get better and for all of us to go home.

At the end of the school day, DeMarco went off to work and I decided to wander a bit. I wanted to see more of the city and get a feel for the place. After walking for a while, I noticed some kids on skateboards, and others who were begging for money and saying they were homeless. I stopped to talk to a guy about my age with a dog. His sign said *Nowhere to live. Can you spare some change?*

"Sorry," I said. "I don't have any money I can give you."

"It's okay, dude. But thanks for stopping."

I petted his dog, a large friendly looking German shepherd. And I couldn't help saying, "I don't quite understand. Why don't you have a place to live? What about your parents?"

He shook his head. "You don't know my parents, bro. I can't live with them. This may not look like fun, but leaving home was the best thing that ever happened to me."

I felt bad for him and wanted to ask more questions, but I knew I'd be intruding on something private and personal. "My dad's in the hospital here. That's why we're in town."

"Sorry to hear that, man."

"I'm staying with my mom in an apartment. Maybe we can help you out."

He shook his head again. "Thanks, but no. Sounds like you have your own grief. I'll be okay. Made it this far. Me and

Genius here." He looked at his dog, and the dog wagged his tail.

"See you around," I said.

"Cheers."

I walked on, thinking about him. Another piece of this large puzzle— life in the city—that just didn't seem to make a whole lot of sense. When I turned the corner near a store that sold musical instruments, I caught something out of the corner of my eye. *No way.*

Yeah. I was being followed. Austin and one of his friends. The one Alexis had said was named Jacob. I turned down another street and, sure enough, they followed. I pretended I hadn't noticed them and kept on walking. There was an old cemetery up ahead. I liked the look of all the big trees and the green grass. I headed in that direction.

Funny how your brain works. I was remembering what my father had taught me about bears—black bears. *If you ever come across one in the woods, leave it alone and back away slowly, giving the bear eye contact. Don't run, because he can outrun you. Don't go in the water, because he can outswim you. And whatever you do, don't climb a tree—for obvious reasons. If the bear doesn't leave you alone, put your arms up in the air to make yourself look larger. Make noises if you have to. If he comes after you, don't lie on the ground—fight back. It's the only thing you can do.*

I'd come across bears in the woods. Not often, but a few times. I could always just back away and they'd leave me alone. Bears don't really want to eat people. They just want to be left alone.

Austin and Jacob were on my trail and getting closer. Maybe going into the cemetery wasn't such a good idea. And I was thinking it was too bad that mean goofs like these guys weren't a little more like bears.

So I stopped and turned. They walked right up to me.

"Visiting dead relatives?" Austin asked.

"Just out for a walk," I said. Jacob circled behind me. "Yeah, we noticed. We thought we'd join you for a stroll."

"No thanks. I'd rather be alone with my thoughts." I shifted my weight and stood so I could see them both, then began to back away over the green grass over the graves.

"A lot of dead people in here," Jacob said. I saw the look in his eyes. It wasn't good.

"I'm just gonna walk away, okay?" I said. I was trying to stay cool, but maybe I sounded too much like a wimp.

"No, it's not okay," Austin said. He lunged at me, but it was easy to shift out of his way. He went down face first. I tried to turn, but Jacob had come up from behind and grabbed my arms.

There were some older people on the walkway not far away, and they were watching. A man was talking into his cell phone.

Austin was getting up off the ground, and I knew I had to make my move if I was going to get away. So I shoved Jacob to break his hold on me. He fell backward and landed hard on the gravestone behind him. I thought I heard something snap as his arm hit the stone. Austin lunged at me again, but he was clumsy and it was easy enough to deflect him and shove him back onto the ground.

I waited. I wanted to finish this and not have to deal with these creeps again. I stood my ground.

Jacob was whimpering now. "You broke my freaking arm." And then: "Somebody help me." Austin started to get to his feet again, and he had venom in his eyes. He was more interested in getting another shot at me than helping his friend. And what if I had really broken Jacob's arm?

So I kept my eyes locked on Austin. "Let's get him some help," I said, trying to be reasonable.

"You're gonna be the one who needs help, asshole," he said. He was reaching into his pocket for something.

That's when I saw a policeman coming through the gates of the cemetery and running our way.

I now had at least two good reasons to get the hell out of there.

So I ran as fast as I could toward the far end of the cemetery and through the gate. The running felt good. But I knew this wasn't over.

Chapter Eight

I'd been afraid before, really afraid. Lost in the forest, stumbling around trying to find my way home. And once, when I was thirteen, all alone and far from home, I'd tripped on a root and ripped open my leg. It was bleeding and it hurt to walk. Somehow my dad found me and carried me home. I asked him how he knew I was hurt and he said he just knew. He said he could see it in his mind. We were that close.

So I understood fear. But nothing like this. I was in a world I didn't understand, and I knew I was in trouble. If Jacob was really hurt, there would be a story. It wouldn't be the true story or the full story, but Austin and Jacob would put the full blame on me. And the police would listen. I'd already been told I'd be in big trouble if I got into another fight. They would charge me with assault this time. I'd been told I was old enough for them to put me in jail. And I knew I couldn't handle that. I could handle the isolation but not being imprisoned. I'd go crazy.

I wanted badly to go to my mom, but the police knew where I lived. And I wanted some advice from my dad, but even if he was awake, I didn't want to trouble him with this.

So I was alone and on my own in the worst kind of wilderness. It was a whole new kind of fear.

I kept walking. I was now far away from the cemetery and circling back toward the library. I found myself in the little park near the fountain and realized I was looking for someone, *anyone*, to help me figure this out. And the only person I could think of was Ernest. It took a while, but I found him. He was sitting in an alley with a couple of his drinking buddies, and he waved when he saw me coming.

They were a ratty-looking pack of unshaven men, some toothless and long-haired, but they seemed more like my kind of people than anyone else in this crazy city. I asked Ernest if he could walk with me for a bit. "Sure thing, Cody boy," he said.

Ernest weaved some as we walked, and I'm sure we looked like an odd pair, but he listened intently to my story. "Jesus, Holy Christ," he said. "Sounds like you're up shit creek without a paddle."

"I can't go to the apartment," I said. "And I can't bring this down on my dad. I don't know what to do."

Ernest seemed a little more clear-headed now and asked if I had any money for coffee.

"Sorry, I don't have a cent."

"But we need coffee. You and me."

I didn't drink coffee, but I needed Ernest, and he sure needed some coffee. I remembered the kid I had met earlier that day. "Okay," I said. "Sit on this bench and let me see what I can do."

I started asking people for change. I got a few nasty looks, but quite a few people were generous. It only took me twenty minutes to get over four dollars. I showed Ernest the money.

"That'll do it," he said.

We went into a Dunkin' Donuts shop and I ordered coffee and some donuts. We sat in a booth and I looked around at the other people. None of them looked like they had the problems I had.

"So what can I do to help?" Ernest asked.

"I need a place to stay," I said. "A place to hide."

"Okay. I can take care of that. But it ain't going to be a four-star hotel."

We lingered in the coffee shop until the manager asked us to leave. Ernest nodded. "I'm used to it, Cody. No big deal. Guess you and I weren't on the invitation list." And then he laughed his funny little laugh that usually ended with a long coughing fit.

Our accommodation for the night was an unlocked shed of sorts beneath an outside stairway. Cardboard boxes lined the floor, and there were a couple of old blankets in there. We didn't go in until the sun had set, and inside it was dark. Very dark. Ernest fell asleep almost instantly. I sat up in the darkness, grieving the loss of my old life, worrying about my fate and, most of all, thinking about my mother and father. It was a long and unhappy night.

Ernest wasn't in good shape in the morning. "I got a headache. My back hurts and my teeth ache," he said. "But none of that is new. What about you, young man? What's next?"

During the night, I'd realized I had to see my parents. "I gotta see my dad," I said. "I gotta make sure he's okay. After that, I don't know."

"You want me to go with you?"

"No. I need to do this on my own." I knew that hauling old Ernest along to the hospital would make us stand out, and I couldn't chance that.

It wasn't difficult to walk into the hospital, take the back stairs up to the cancer ward and go into my dad's room without being noticed. My mom was there with him, holding his hand, and she looked worried. When she saw me, she gasped, jumped up and gave me a crushing hug. "Thank God," she said. My dad was awake and propped up in bed but looking weak. I walked over to him and gave him a hug.

"The police came," my mom said. "More trouble. They want to question you."

I explained what had happened and said I was sorry for not coming home. My dad watched me gravely as I told my story. "What should I do?" I asked, looking at Mom and then at Dad.

My dad motioned me nearer. I leaned in close to him. I don't know if it was the cancer or the drugs he had been given, but something had given him a hollow look. His eyes were glazed, and he was breathing funny.

"Cody," he said, pausing to take two deep breaths. "You have to leave here. You have to go home." I looked over at my mom, who was now crying. She nodded in agreement.

We sat together in silence for a few minutes as it began to sink in. I didn't want to leave them. But there was nothing I could do to help them. And if I stayed and was arrested, it would only cause them more grief. I wanted to scream or cry, but I held back everything and remained silent.

I gave my dad another big hug. "I'll be okay," I said. "You always said I had good survival skills."

My mom kissed me on the neck. "Be careful," she told me.

As I slipped out the door, I felt like I was abandoning them forever, but I knew I had to try to get back home.

As I walked down the hallway, I saw a police officer at the far end, speaking to a nurse. I had no way of knowing if he was looking for me, but I wasn't about to chance walking past him.

I opened the stairwell door and heard footsteps coming up the stairs. Before I could turn back, I saw that it was DeMarco and Alexis.

Chapter Nine

"What are you guys doing here?" I asked.

"You didn't show up at school," DeMarco said, "so I talked to Costanzo. He said the police were looking for you. Was it Austin again?"

"Yeah. And Jacob. I think I may have broken his arm."

"Are you joking?" Alexis said.

"I didn't mean to. What's with those two anyway?"

DeMarco shook his head. "They've been like that ever since I can remember. I could always get them to lighten up on me. But you, Cody, you must've pushed all the wrong buttons."

I took a gulp of air. "Look. I've realized something. I don't belong here. I don't belong in your school and I don't belong in this city. I'm leaving."

"Where are you gonna go?" Alexis asked, real concern in her voice.

"Home. Where else can I go?"

"But your parents are here, Cody," DeMarco said. "You'd be all alone out there in the woods."

"I can take care of myself."

"How are you going to get there?" Alexis asked.

"I don't know," I admitted.

"We'll go with you," DeMarco said. "We'll figure something out." Alexis looked me in the eye and nodded.

"I don't know," I said. "But let's get out of here before someone comes looking for me."

We walked down the stairs, through the crowded lobby and out into the bright, cool morning. "Good day for an adventure," Alexis said, trying to put a good spin on it. "I say we get down to the harbor and take the ferry first. That will get you out of town, Cody, and headed in the right direction. We'll figure out something from there."

"Sure." I'd seen the ferry from the bridge over the harbor when we had first come into the city. The ferry was just the first leg of the journey. Once we got to the other side, we'd have to find a bus that would take us part of the way down the shore. But after that we'd be on our own. We'd have to hitchhike maybe.

Alexis guided us to the waterfront and paid for all of us to get on the ferry. We walked around the boat on the outside deck, and I breathed in the sweet salt air. It was intoxicating. I felt better already. DeMarco stood looking over the rail and down into the water. Alexis was studying me. "So that's what you look like when you smile," she said.

"Was I smiling?"

"Well, you didn't have that beaten-dog look you've been wearing."

The ferry began to move away from the dock. The motion felt good. I was going home. "I'd never be able to fit in here."

"You're not alone," Alexis said. "I know I'm not the same as you, but I've felt that way most of my life. So I stopped trying."

"But you grew up here. Your home is here."

"It doesn't matter."

I started to walk to the back of the ferry. Alexis and DeMarco followed. We watched as the buildings of the city grew smaller in the distance. "Ever since my dad got sick, everything changed. First he said it was nothing, that he was going to be all right. But he kept getting worse. Against his wishes, my mom took him to a doctor. He had some tests. Then we had to come here. He hated making us leave our home and come to the city."

"What were your parents thinking anyway?" Alexis asked. "When they moved so far away and dropped out of everything?"

"It was before I was born. They were very idealistic. They wanted to live a simple life. I heard my dad's speech a million times. They didn't want to be corrupted by money or possessions— anything more than what they needed to survive. My dad would say, *We don't want to be a burden to the planet*. I know that sounds whacked. But you don't know my parents. We grew most of our own food. My dad homeschooled me. He had to write up reports for the government, but everyone pretty much left us alone."

"I think it sounds amazing," Alexis said. "I mean, I know all kinds of people who claim to be environmentally aware, but they're all hypocrites. Even me."

"For them it's more than that. It's like a religion, I guess. They were trying to live according to what they believed. Self-sufficiency, being at one with nature, avoiding what my dad would call *all the corruption of modern living.*"

"Man, that's some heavy shit," DeMarco said. "I don't think I've ever met people like that. Must be kind of weird being raised by a couple of saints."

"Well, they aren't exactly perfect, but they *are* unique. They've lived what they truly believe to be right. That's the only life I know. And they've taught me well. They've taught me to be true to myself."

"Amen," DeMarco said. "What else did they teach you?"

"Survival skills. Good survival skills. The only problem is, the rules of survival in the city are a whole lot different from the rules of wilderness survival."

DeMarco looked serious. "So if we get to your old homestead, Cody, you might have to teach us some of those survival skills. I'm assuming you can't walk to the corner 7-Eleven for a snack whenever you feel like it. We gonna have to fight off bears or what?"

"You don't fight with bears, believe me." I turned and smiled at him. But as I looked over his shoulder through the window of the inside passenger area, something caught my eye.

It was Ernest, slumped over in a seat.

Chapter Ten

Because it was the middle of the day, there were only a handful of other passengers in the seating area. DeMarco and Alexis followed me inside. Just like Ernest to conk out again somewhere in public, I thought. I shook him gently at first but didn't get a response. I shook a little harder, "Ernest, are you okay?"

His eyes slowly opened, and he looked frightened. Then he realized it was me. "Cody. Jesus, lad. At first I thought you were my father. I must have been dreaming."

"Do I look like your father?" I joked, relieved the guy had just been asleep and not dead.

He took a deep breath and tried to straighten himself up. "No. It was just the dream. But the damn man keeps showing up when I sleep. When I was a kid, he beat the crap out of me on a regular basis. Nothing I ever did was good enough for him. And he told me so. He still haunts me, the old goon, even though he's dead."

I introduced DeMarco and Alexis.

"Shouldn't you hoodlums be in school?" Ernest asked.

I explained my current problems.

"Running away from shit like that usually doesn't work. It's like running from my old man. He always caught up with me. He still catches up with me."

I guess I rolled my eyes a bit. Look who was giving me advice.

"I wanted to get the hell out of the city too. But the farther away I went, the more lost I felt. So I came back. Not much of a life, I guess, but at least I know my way around."

"What are you doing on the ferry?" Alexis asked. "Where are you going?"

He laughed. "Oh, I'm not going anywhere. It's a cheap ride. I like the feel of the water under the boat. I get to sleep. Usually I can go back and forth a few times before they put me ashore. They all know me, so they leave me alone unless someone complains."

The ferry was coming into the dock on the other side of the harbor now. I'd never experienced anything quite like it before. I thought for a second we were going to crash, we were moving so fast, but whoever was steering cut the engines and we glided to a stop right beside the dock. Some people were standing there, waiting to get on board. One of them was a cop. I nodded to DeMarco.

He saw that I was about to make a run for it, out the door and past the cop. He grabbed my wrist. "Be cool," he said.

The doors opened and we moved toward the ramp off the ferry. I watched as the policeman walked through the exiting passengers and headed our way. I was still ready to bolt, but then I realized he was ignoring us and focusing on Ernest.

Ernest knew what was coming.

"You'll have to go ashore," the cop said. "You know how it goes."

Ernest nodded. "Yes, Officer."

So the four of us walked off together. The cop followed, but once we were out of the ferry terminal, he headed down the street. Ernest let out a big sigh. He pulled an empty booze bottle from his coat pocket and deposited it in a recycling can. "Guess I'll have to walk the bridge back to town," he said. "It's a good day for a hike. See the sights, get some fresh air." Then he let out his loud, unhealthy, signature cough.

We stood silently there by the water for a minute. Ernest was just staring up into the sky when he started talking. "Cody, is your home that nice little hobbit hut in the woods, or is your home where your parents are and"—he nodded at Alexis and DeMarco—"where your friends are?"

I didn't say anything, but his words were getting to me. I really did want to see my home again, but what was I going to do when I got there? And what was I *really* running from? I was running because I was afraid, not because I'd really done anything wrong.

And then Ernest drove the point home. "What if you run off and something happens to your dad in the hospital and you're not there? They wouldn't even be able to get in touch with you."

I looked at Alexis, and she nodded. DeMarco looked at me and said, "It's your call, Codeman."

The ferry had not left yet. "I've got some more money," Alexis said. "Enough to get us all back across the harbor."

I nodded at Ernest. "C'mon. Let's go."

"You guys go. They won't let me back on today. Like I said, it's a good day for a walk." And then he shook my hand and looked into my eyes. "Do whatever needs to be done, brother. And take care of those parents. They're the only ones you've got." Then he turned and began to walk toward the bridge. The ferry sounded its horn, and Alexis slapped my arm. "Let's go, Cody."

The three of us got back on the ferry, and almost immediately it left the dock. We stood outside at the front of the boat, watching as the city grew larger in front of us.

"What are you going to do?" DeMarco asked.

"Guess I'll just go straight to the police. Tell them my side of the story."

"We'll go with you," Alexis said.

When I walked through the doors of the police station for the second time, I feared I might never walk back out. But Alexis and DeMarco were with me, and I had faith in them.

I told the desk cop who I was, why I was there and that I wanted to talk to someone about it. He looked me up on his computer. "Says here you were involved in some kind of fight at your school. I don't see anything else."

Austin and Jacob had not reported what happened in the cemetery. "But I feel like I should talk to someone and explain what happened next," I said.

The cop didn't seem that interested. "We're pretty busy around here," he said, even though it didn't look busy at all. "Why don't you go back to school?"

I felt like a weight had been lifted off me. I guess I had not badly injured Jacob after all. Maybe he and Austin would still try to get back at me, but I wouldn't fight them again. I'd find ways to stay clear of them, to get them off my case. I'd use my wits instead of my strength. It was all about a new set of survival skills.

Chapter Eleven

Mr. Costanzo spotted us as soon as we walked in the door. He had his arms folded in front of his chest. "Why aren't you all in class?" he asked.

"We were just headed to class, Mr. Costanzo," DeMarco said. "Cody said he needed some fresh air, and we thought we'd better stay with him so he wouldn't get lost, being new here and all."

It wasn't what he said but the way he said it—smooth, respectful. DeMarco was impressive at deflecting trouble. Maybe I did need to learn from him.

"Sorry we lost track of time, sir," I said. "We'd like to go to class now."

Just then Mr. Costanzo's cell phone rang. He looked at it, then us. He waved his hand for us to go.

"You going to be okay?" Alexis asked me as we walked down the hall.

"I don't know," I answered. "I just really don't seem to belong here. I still don't understand the rules or know how to act." Being back in the school building had me rattled already. Costanzo had been right there as if he was waiting for us. I didn't look forward to going to the classroom and having kids stare at me again like I was the freak from the woods.

"I'm sorry about what I did to you the other day," Alexis said. "I like you now that I know you. I think I understand a bit better. I'd like to get to know you a little more."

DeMarco smiled. "Guess I can't compete with that," he joked.

"I want to meet your mom and dad," Alexis said. "My parents are morons. Yours sound like heroes. Can I meet them?"

"Sure," I said.

"Gotta go," she said. "My class is on the other side of the building." Then she kissed me on the cheek and ran down the hall. She did it like it wasn't a big deal. But it was. Aside from my mom, no one had ever kissed me. The feeling booted the gloom right out of my head.

"Loverboy, we gotta get you to math class. We're already late."

"You go," I said. "I've really gotta pee. It's been a long day. I'll see you there."

"Sure thing. Don't get lost." As DeMarco walked on, I dipped into the boys' washroom. Somebody else was right behind me, but he went straight into a toilet stall.

I was standing at the urinal, taking the longest leak of my life. My head was full of a jumble of things, and I wondered if I'd ever be able to settle into life here at the school. That's when I heard the toilet-stall door open. I zipped up and turned around.

It was Austin, glaring at me. He angled toward the main door and just stood there, blocking my way out. We were alone in here. I studied the look on his face. I couldn't quite figure it out. Anger? Hatred? Since coming to the city, I'd realized that other people communicated by the way they looked at you. I couldn't read many of those expressions. This one especially puzzled me. Nastiness, yes. Animosity, for sure. Threatening, definitely. But there were traces of something else. It was a look that said he didn't approve of anyone or anything. It was the look of someone who didn't even like himself.

"Just you and me this time," he said. His breathing was heavy.

"I'm not gonna do this," I said.

"Afraid to fight?"

"We've been through this," I said. "It's pointless."

"You hurt Jacob. He had X-rays. Nothing was broken, but you sure messed up his arm."

"I didn't mean to."

"So you're sorry you did it?"

"Yeah," I said, "I'm sorry I did it. I just want this crap to end."

"Saying you're sorry doesn't quite make things all right." Austin moved toward me, but I didn't move. He had his right hand in his jacket pocket. I wasn't sure what that was about. But I was ready for him to make the first move. I decided that when he went for me, I'd push him off and get the hell out of there, go straight to Costanzo if I had to. But I was not going to hit him.

"Where the hell are you from anyway? And why the hell did you move here?"

I decided to tell him the truth. "We lived a long way from here. Just my family and me. I'm here because my dad got real sick. Cancer. We had to get him to the hospital."

Austin didn't seem to know how to respond to that. "So you think everyone should feel sorry for you, right?"

"No," I said. "I'd just be happy to be left alone. I don't want anyone to feel sorry for me."

Austin took his hand out of his pocket. "How is he?" he asked in a different voice. It wasn't what I was expecting to hear.

"I'm not sure," I said. "He doesn't seem to be getting better."

"Hospitals suck," Austin said.

"This one's not so bad. It just seems that the treatment is wearing him down more."

"Yeah. I think sometimes doctors do more harm than good."

"What do you mean?"

"I hate hospitals."

"You spent some time there? You were sick?"

Austin backed away and leaned against one of the sinks. Behind him I could see our reflection in the bathroom mirror. "My mom had cancer when I was ten. She died in a hospital. I think it was that place that killed her." Austin now looked like a hurt little kid. All the anger had left him.

"I'm sorry," I said.

But then he sucked in some air, puffed out his chest and glared at me. "Screw off, asshole," he shouted. "Just screw off." Then he grabbed the door, slammed it hard against the wall as he opened it, and walked out.

I was left looking at my reflection and thinking that maybe some stuff was starting to make a bit of sense after all.

Chapter Twelve

By the time school was over, I was tired. Sleeping on the street sucks. I thought about Ernest and the life he was living. DeMarco slapped me on the back as he jogged by. He was on his way to his afternoon job. "Stay out of trouble, Cody," he told me as he scooted by. "And lighten up, brother. Be cool."

I saw Austin and Jacob. They saw me, too, but Austin just walked away. Jacob followed him. I was in a bit of a fog—tired, still a bit confused, attempting to put all the pieces together. I was trying to understand my new identity, and it was beginning to click that even though I'd only been here a short while, I was now connected to other people— DeMarco, Alexis, Ernest, even Austin. It was a new feeling for me.

Drifting out of my fog, I realized someone was following me. I turned to see Alexis walking quickly toward me. "Wait up," she said. "You said you would introduce me to your parents."

I was on my way to the hospital, but today didn't seem like the right day. I was going to have to explain to my parents what had happened. I really wanted to have a heart-to-heart talk with my dad. The truth was, I was really worried about him.

"Can we do that some other time?" I said.

Alexis looked hurt. "So this is how you do it? You draw me in and then you push me away?"

Once again, I realized I didn't understand much of anything when it came to communication.

"I'm just not sure my dad's in any shape to see visitors," I said.

Alexis stopped and stood there on the sidewalk with her arms folded. I stopped walking and turned to look at her. "Don't you get it?" she asked.

"Get what?"

"I know that you're going through a rough time. I understand that your dad is really sick. I think you need more than just you to see this thing through. That's why DeMarco and I were willing to run away with you."

"So you feel sorry for me? That's why you want to hang out with me?"

"Yeah, I feel bad about what's going on in your life. But there's more than that."

I wasn't sure I liked having people pity me, not even a girl like Alexis. But I wasn't going to push her away. I told her about my encounter with Austin.

"Some people want sympathy for their pain," she said. "Some just want to push it onto others."

"Come on," I said. "Let's go to the hospital. I actually could use some company. I'm really worried about my dad."

"I promise I'll be good," she said.

Alexis could see I was feeling panicky as we walked into the lobby of the hospital. She took my hand and squeezed it hard. We took the elevator up to the cancer ward, and I led her to my dad's room.

When we walked in, my mom was crying. My dad was not in the bed. I felt the blood drain out of my face.

"Mom?"

"It's your father," she said, then started to cry some more.

I held her in my arms. "What about him? What happened?"

"He's so stubborn," she said.

"What do you mean?"

Just then my dad walked into the room. He had his old clothes on, and he leaned against the doorframe. He looked very, very sick. "Cody, I'm going home. We're all going home." But as he stepped toward me, he started to falter, so I grabbed him and helped him to the bed.

Alexis didn't say a word. She slipped to the side of the room and sat down in a chair.

"Convince him he has to stay here," Mom said.

My dad was breathing heavily as he leaned back on the bed. I'd never seen him look so bad.

He noticed Alexis now but didn't acknowledge her presence. Instead, he stared intently at me. "Why did you come back?" he asked.

"It's all okay. There was a misunderstanding. I'm not in any real trouble."

"It doesn't matter. I need to get out of here and go back home. This hospital is killing me."

I thought about what Austin had said about his mom. Maybe Dad was right. But he didn't look like he was in any shape to travel anywhere. There was a terrible stillness in the room. All I could hear was my father's labored breathing.

"Cody," he said. "We always lived what we believed, right?

"Yeah."

"We believed in being self-sufficient, taking care of ourselves, not being a burden to anyone or anything. Not being dependent on anyone but us."

"You taught me those things," I said. "And more."

"Live what you believe in."

"I know."

"But being here is all wrong. Everything feels wrong. And I don't think I'm getting any better."

Then he paused, swallowed hard and said the thing I was most afraid he would say. "If I'm going to die, I'd rather die at home."

My mom burst into tears again.

I looked over at Alexis and saw the shock in her eyes. She didn't say a word. My father's statement echoed inside my head, and my mind rebelled at the thought. I felt like screaming. And I suddenly knew then that if my father was stubborn enough, we would go home. And he would likely die there.

And I couldn't let that happen.

"Help me up, Cody. Help me get downstairs." There was determination in his eyes, but also desperation.

"No," my mom said. "Don't do it."

Chapter Thirteen

Alexis looked quite upset now, and I guessed she was wishing she hadn't stumbled into my family drama. My mom wasn't in any shape to improve the situation, so I knew it was up to me.

"Dad," I said. "You taught me a lot of things about survival, and you always seemed to be right."

He nodded and tried to get up again but didn't quite have the energy. He looked annoyed with me. "You going to give me a lecture, Cody? If so, save it." I had rarely heard my father sound so stern.

I decided to continue. "You always told me that if I got truly lost in the woods, the most important thing was to stay put and not get more lost."

"Right, but we're not in the woods."

"I think we are."

He said nothing.

"You said to stay put, stay calm, assess the situation. Come up with a strategy."

"That's why we're going home," he insisted.

I shook my head. "Dad, we're lost, all right, but if we leave here, we'll be more lost."

My mom got up and stood on the other side of the bed, leaned over and gave my father a hug. "Listen to Cody, please."

My dad lay back in the bed now. "Looks like I'm outnumbered," he said. "So I guess you're in charge, are you, Son?"

I shrugged. "I'm just trying to make sure we all get out of the woods safe and sound."

My dad's breathing was a bit steadier now. He looked at Alexis and then at me.

"This is Alexis," I said. "A friend. A good friend."

Alexis gave a funny little-girl wave to my dad.

And then he closed his eyes. He smiled a bit and let out a short little laugh.

My dad did get worse after that. Much worse. For a while we were fairly certain he would die. The doctors had tried chemo and radiation, and they just dragged him further down. But they didn't give up on him. The worst for me was seeing my once-strong dad weakened and finally giving up on himself. A bone-marrow transplant came next, and at first that didn't seem to do any good either. And it caused him a lot of pain.

I wished I could take on some of that pain myself and ease his burden. I couldn't stand to see him suffer.

Alexis insisted on coming to the hospital with me almost every day. It wasn't easy for her, but she always seemed to be there for me.

One Saturday when she was walking with me to the hospital, I said, "I don't get it. Why do you want to do this? This is not your problem. I'm sure it's no fun for you to hang out with my mom and me at the hospital on a day when you could be doing whatever you want to do."

"This is what I want to do. And I'm not sure why it seems so important to me. But it is. Maybe because I've had it pretty easy in life. Nobody in my family has ever had to face what you're dealing with. But then, my family... well, it's never really felt like a family. Not like you guys. We all just live in the same house. My father travels a lot. My mother is more interested in her friends and social life than in us. And I always feel like an outsider in my own home."

"That's awful," I said.

"When I see you with your parents, I feel the bond that's there. And that's something pretty precious. But more than that, I want to be there for you."

I think it was at that moment that I realized I no longer felt lost in the city. Alexis had found me stumbling around in the urban wilderness and had known the way out, the way back to safety, the way home.

Although I worried about my father, I settled into a routine at school. I became old news, and kids mostly ignored me. I ran into Austin a few times and said hi, but he just ignored me. He had stopped hanging out with Jacob and mostly wandered the halls between classes, looking angry and alone.

One day at lunchtime, I walked over to the park across the street to get some fresh air and look at the trees. I heard some noises and walked off the path to find Jacob sitting on top of Austin, beating the crap out of him. I came up behind Jacob, wrapped my arms around him in a powerful bear hug, picked him off Austin and held him in that grip. He started to scream at me.

Austin's nose was bleeding, and I figured he'd had the wind knocked out of him. He was having a hard time breathing as he got to his feet.

Jacob finally broke free and spun around on his heels, ready to smash whoever had interfered. When he saw it was me, he stopped himself. "Screw you, asshole," he said and then spit a big gob right in my face. As he started to walk away, I almost grabbed him again. But I didn't. I let him go and wiped my face.

Austin was holding his hand to his nose, trying to stop the bleeding. He'd gotten his breath back but looked totally whipped.

"You okay?" I asked.

"Why'd you do that?" he asked.

I just shrugged. I was thinking about what he'd told me, about his mom dying in the hospital when he was young.

He looked at me for a long, weird minute, then said, "How's your dad?"

"I don't know. He's still in the hospital. They haven't given up on him yet."

Austin just kept staring at me. What I saw in that look was the face of a lost little boy, a kid who really hurt. Not just from being beat up, but from something

Lesley Choyce

deeper in him, some pain that wouldn't disappear. "I hope he gets better," Austin said. And then he walked away.

Later that day, Alexis walked with me to the hospital. As we went by the library, we saw Ernest, passed out on the bench again. Alexis helped me prop him up. It took me a while to wake him up.

At first he looked scared, until he could get my face into focus. "Cody?"

"Yeah. You okay?"

"Do I look okay?"

"Nope. You look bad. You got to cut this out." I thought about guys like Jacob, maybe even Austin, finding an old geezer passed out like this. If they thought they could get away with it, they'd kick him or beat him or maybe even light him on fire. I'd been following the news recently and was shocked at how mean and cruel some

102

people could be, even some of the kids from my school.

Ernest studied Alexis's worried face and seemed to see something there. He turned to me.

"What?" I asked. "What can we do to help?" I'd asked him that before, but he'd always said he was okay and didn't need anyone's help. Now something had changed.

"I need a couple of weeks away from here to sober up."

"What do you mean, *away from here*?" Alexis asked.

"If I stay here, I do the same old routine every day. It's what I know. It's just what I do. But if I could get myself away and be alone, I can work on this. I think I can change."

I had a bright idea. "You want to go live somewhere in the woods, like I did?"

His face lit up. "Yeah."

"You're serious?"

"I think I am. Cody—I'm gonna die here. I can feel it. One of these times, I'm not gonna wake up."

"But if you go off on your own, somewhere in the sticks, there won't be anyone around to help if you need help."

"Yes. That's just it. I think that if there is no one to rely on but me... I think I can do it."

"You think you can handle living somewhere way out in the woods, completely off the grid?"

"Kid, I've been off the grid for years."

I was thinking I should ask my parents before I offered, but I had a gut feeling I might not have another chance. By the next time I saw Ernest, he might be back on the bottle and not wanting to change. Or he might be dead. So I told him he could stay at my old home. For now, at least.

He didn't think I was serious at first, but then he began to smile.

"The house is unlocked. There's food there. And a well out back. But it's a long way away. And, like I said, there's nobody around if you need help."

"Like *I* said, I really need to be alone. I need to do this by myself."

I really didn't know if an alcoholic like Ernest could go cold turkey. I knew it wouldn't be easy—maybe it was even impossible. But I was willing to give him a chance. I started to explain how to get there, but he looked puzzled, so I tore a piece of paper from my school notebook and carefully drew a map.

Alexis opened her bag and took out some money. "Go down to the terminal and take the bus. Get something to eat first," she added.

I pointed at my map. "Just so you know, the bus will only take you as far as here," I said, indicating the town nearest to where I'd lived. "You'll have to walk the rest of the way."

"I can walk," Ernest said. He looked very determined.

And then he gave Alexis a hug. And he looked me straight in the eye and shook my hand.

"You guys are great," he said. "I'll see you in two weeks."

As he walked off toward the bus station, Alexis suddenly looked worried. "I gave him fifty dollars. Do you think he'll blow it on booze?"

"Maybe," I said. "But maybe not."

Chapter Fourteen

Three weeks after the bone-marrow transplant, my dad started to show a little color in his skin. He started to have an appetite. He was sitting upright when Alexis and I arrived in the room. He was starting to look like my old dad. And he started giving me lectures again. Some of the same old themes but also some additions. A lot of the old philosophy and idealism. But something else too. "Sometimes, Cody, the hardest thing you can do is let other people help you when you're down and out," he said. And I think I fully understood what he meant.

The day finally came when my dad was allowed to leave the hospital. I'd like to say he looked cured and healthy, but he had lost a lot of weight, and he was pale and a bit shaky as he walked. "He'll slowly regain his strength," the young doctor said. "But we've done everything we can do. He needs rest, and he needs to be home."

It was hard to say goodbye to Alexis, but I knew I needed to be with my mom and dad. And I too wanted to be home. Except for Alexis and DeMarco, there wasn't anything about school that I would miss. Alexis promised she'd come visit.

"How are you gonna do that?"

"I memorized your map. I'll take the bus and then I'll walk if I have to. I'll call you."

I gave her a soft, sad look and a half smile. She understood. I didn't have a phone.

"Don't worry. I'll just show up."

My dad was a bit weepy on the trip to our old homestead. It felt weird to be on our way back to a world we had left behind, one that seemed a million miles from my life in the city and going to school. I hadn't heard a word from Ernest, but I had told my parents about him. I knew it was possible he might still be there and that we might find him drunk or maybe even dead.

But we were going home.

When we arrived, walking the final leg of our long trail through the forest, I watched my dad taking deep breaths and seemingly getting stronger with each step.

When we opened the door to the house, there was no one inside. There was no sign of Ernest, just a note on the table.

Welcome back home, Cody. Mission accomplished.
Ernest

Lesley Choyce divides his time between teaching, writing, running Pottersfield Press and hosting a television talk show. He is the author of almost sixty books for youth and adults. Lesley lives in Lawrencetown Beach, Nova Scotia.

orca soundings

For more information on all the books
in the Orca Soundings series, please visit
www.orcabook.com.